PEACHTREE

TWO CAN

First dictionary

Copyright © 2005 Two-Can Publishing

Two-Can Publishing
An imprint of Creative Publishing international, Inc.
18705 Lake Drive East
Chanhassen, MN 55317
1-800-328-3895
www.two-canpublishing.com

Created by Bookwork Limited
Unit 17, Piccadilly Mill, Lower Street, Stroud,
Gloucestershire, GL5 2HT

Literacy consultant: Nicola Morgan

ISBN 1-58728-439-1

Library of Congress Cataloging-in-Publication Data
Two-Can first dictionary: the essential first word book for young readers.
    p. cm.
  ISBN 1-58728-439-1
  1. English language—Dictionaries, Juvenile. I. Title: First dicitonary. II.
Two-Can (Firm)
  PE1628.5.T88 2005
  423—dc22
                                                          2004008920

        1 2 3 4 5 6 09 08 07 06 05 04

                    Printed in Malaysia

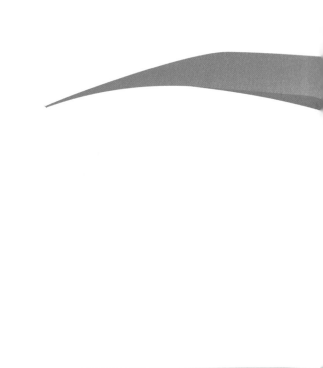

First

TWO CAN

dictionary

How to Use This Book

This book is a dictionary. A dictionary tells you what words mean and shows you how to spell them. This dictionary has more than 500 words that you can look up. They are listed in alphabetical order. Words that begin with **a** come first, and words that begin with **z** come last. There are 26 letters in the alphabet.

Dictionaries can help you discover new words. They can also tell you new things about words you already know.

How to find a word

If you want to look up a word that you have heard, think of what letter it begins with, such as **t** for **tent**. Then look for the first page that has a **t** in a purple circle at the top. Try to guess the next letter in the word, such as the **e** in **tent**. Then go through the list of **t** words until you find those beginning **te**, and so on. The words are in alphabetical order, so words that begin **ta** will come before words that begin **te**.

More than one meaning

Some words have more than one meaning. In a dictionary, each meaning of a word has its own explanation. This explanation is called a definition. In this book, different definitions of a word have a space between them, so you will know where a new one begins.

Different kinds of words

Different kinds of words do different things. In this dictionary, there are nouns, adjectives, and verbs. A noun is the name of something, such as a **farm**. An adjective, such as **fat**, is a word that describes a noun. A verb is a doing word, such as **feel**. This book tells you what kind of word each one is. Some words can be more than one kind of word. The word **cut** is both a noun and a verb. Each form of the word gets its own definition.

farm (noun)
A **farm** is a place where farmers grow plants or raise animals for food.

fat (adjective)
Fat is the opposite of thin. Someone who eats too much may get fat.

feel (verb)
You **feel** something when you touch it. It may feel rough or smooth.

Looking at a definition

Below is a picture of two pages from this dictionary. Above and below the picture are some labels. These labels show you where to find some of the features explained on this page. Read these labels before you get started. Then turn the page and start exploring hundreds of words and their meanings!

bzzzzzzzzzz zzzzzzzz

This word, in large, black letters, is the word you are looking up

This circle shows you what letter the words on this page begin with.

The kind of word you are looking up is shown in parentheses here.

| a | b | c | d | **e** **f** | g | h | i | j | k | l | m | n | o | p | q | r | s | t | u | v | w | x | y | z |

Ee

eagle (noun)
An **eagle** is a large bird with sharp claws and a hooked beak. Eagles catch and eat other animals.

Earth (noun)
Earth is the planet on which we live. It is round and travels around the sun. Most of Earth is covered with water. There are large areas of land, too.

The soil that plants grow in is also called **earth**.

easy (adjective)
If something is **easy** to do, you can do it without any problems. Easy is the opposite of difficult.

eat (verb)
When you **eat**, you put food in your mouth, chew it, and swallow it. You must eat food to stay alive.

egg (noun)
An **egg** is an oval or round object in which young animals grow until they are ready to be born. Female birds lay eggs. Most female amphibians, fish, reptiles, and insects lay eggs, too.

Earth

electricity (noun)
Electricity is power that travels through wires into our homes. You use electricity when you switch on a light.

elephant (noun)
An **elephant** is a large mammal with a long nose called a trunk. Elephants live in forests and grassy areas of Asia and Africa. They can live for 70 years.

engine (noun)
Some machines have **engines**. This part makes power to run the machine. Cars have engines.

Europe (noun)
Europe is a large area of land. It is a continent. France and Spain are two of the many countries in Europe.

20

Ff

face (noun)
Your **face** is the front part of your head, from your forehead to your chin.

face (verb)
When you **face** something, you look toward it.

fall (verb)
To **fall** is to land suddenly on the floor or ground. You may hurt yourself.

family (noun) plural **families**
A **family** is a group of people made up of grandparents, parents and children. Some families have aunts, uncles, and cousins too. Who is in your family?

farm (noun)
A **farm** is a place where farmers grow plants or raise animals for food.

fast (adjective)
A **fast** runner runs quickly. Fast is the opposite of slow.

fat (adjective)
Fat is the opposite of thin. Someone who eats too much may get fat.

favorite (adjective)
When you like something best, it is your **favorite**. What is your favorite color?

feather (noun)
A **feather** is one of the long, thin objects that cover a bird's body. Feathers keep a bird warm and help it to fly through the air.

feel (verb)
You **feel** something when you touch it. It may feel rough or smooth.

You can also use the word **feel** to say how you are inside. You may feel happy or sad, tired or hungry.

fence (noun)
A **fence** is a kind of wall made of wood, metal or wire. Some fences keep people out. Some fences keep animals in.

21

A new meaning for a word starts after an empty space.

Usually, a noun is made plural by adding an s. (Plural means more than one.) Here you can see if the plural form of a word is spelled another way.

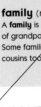

Aa

add (verb)
When you **add** something, you put it together with other things to make more. If you have two eggs and you add one more, you will have three.

Africa (noun)
Africa is a huge area of land. It is a continent with more than 50 countries.

age (noun)
Your **age** is how old you are.

air (noun)
Air is all around you, but you cannot see it. Air is what you breathe.

airplane (noun)
An **airplane** is a machine that has wings and an engine, and flies through the air. People travel in an airplane to go long distances quickly.

alphabet (noun)
An **alphabet** is all the letters used in writing. You can see the English alphabet along the top of these pages.

amphibian (noun)
An **amphibian** is an animal that lives in the water when young but lives on land as an adult. Frogs and toads are amphibians. Their young are called tadpoles.

an airplane

Aa

angry (adjective)
If you are **angry,** you feel mad. You may want to yell.

animal (noun)
An **animal** is a living thing that can move on its own. Fish and birds are animals. So are you!

ant (noun)
An **ant** is a kind of small insect. Ants live in a large group called a colony.

Antarctica (noun)
Antarctica is a large area of land. It is a continent at the bottom of Earth, around the South Pole. It is covered with a thick layer of ice.

apple (noun)
An **apple** is a round fruit. It is crisp and juicy, with red, green, or yellow skin.

Arctic (noun)
The **Arctic** is a very cold part of Earth around the North Pole. It is at the opposite end of Earth from Antarctica. Thick ice floats on the sea there.

Asia (noun)
Asia is a huge area of land. It is the largest continent on Earth. More than half the world's people live in Asia.

astronaut (noun)
An **astronaut** is someone who travels into space in a spaceship. Would you like to be an astronaut?

aunt (noun)
If your mother or father has a sister, she is your **aunt**. If either of them has a brother, his wife is your aunt, too. You may have lots of aunts!

Australia (noun)
Australia is a large area of land. It is a continent. It is also the name of the large country on that continent.

autumn (noun)
Autumn is the time of year between summer and winter. Leaves fall off of some trees in autumn. The weather becomes cooler.

Bb

baby (noun) plural **babies**
A **baby** is a very young child.

bake (verb)
To **bake** is to cook something in the oven. You bake a cake to cook it.

ball (noun)
A **ball** is a round object. In some sports, you kick, hit, throw, or bounce a ball.

A **ball** is also a large, fancy party where people dance. Cinderella met her prince at a ball.

balloon (noun)
A **balloon** is a colored rubber bag that you fill with air or a kind of gas called helium to make it float in the air. Some balloons are so large they can lift a basket full of people into the sky.

banana (noun)
A **banana** is a long, curved fruit with a thick, yellow skin. You must peel off the skin before you eat the banana.

bang (noun)
A **bang** is a sudden loud noise. A balloon often pops with a loud bang.

bark (noun)
Bark is the hard material that covers the trunk and branches of a tree.

bark (verb)
To **bark** is what a dog does when it makes a loud noise in its throat.

bath (noun)
When you take a **bath,** you sit in a tub of water and wash yourself. You may add bubble bath to make the water bubble up and smell nice.

bear (noun)
A **bear** is a wild mammal. It is large and strong and has thick fur. Many bears are fierce.

beautiful (adjective)
You say something is **beautiful** if you enjoy looking at it. You may also think something sounds beautiful or smells beautiful.

bed (noun)
A **bed** is a piece of furniture that you lie on to rest or sleep. You probably have a bed in your bedroom.

bee (noun)
A **bee** is a kind of insect that has wings. It makes a buzzing noise as it flies. A honeybee has black stripes. It may sting you if you bother it.

bicycle (noun)
A **bicycle** is a machine that you can ride. It has two wheels and two pedals for your feet.

big (adjective)
Another word for **big** is large. Big is the opposite of small.

bird (noun)
A **bird** is an animal with wings, feathers, and a beak. Most birds can fly.

a bee

bzzzzzzzzzzzzzz

begin (verb)
When you start to do something, you **begin**. When you start a new book, you begin at the beginning.

bell (noun)
A **bell** is a metal object that you hit or shake to produce a ringing sound. You may have a round bell on your bicycle.

bend (noun)
If something has a **bend** in it, it is not straight. A road that goes around a curve has a bend in it.

bend (verb)
To **bend** something is to make it not straight. You can bend a piece of wire. You can bend your arm at the elbow.

birthday (noun)
Your **birthday** is the special day every year when you remember the day you were born. You may have a party.

bite (verb)
To **bite** is to use your teeth to cut into something. You bite a cookie to eat it.

blind (adjective)

A **blind** person cannot see.

blood (noun)

Blood is the red liquid that flows through your body. If you cut yourself, some blood may come out.

boat (noun)

A **boat** is a vehicle that floats. Boats carry people and goods across water.

body (noun) plural **bodies**

Your **body** is all of you. Your arms, legs, and head are parts of your body.

bone (noun)

A **bone** is one of the hard white parts inside an animal's body that makes up its skeleton. You have nearly 300 bones inside you.

book (noun)

A **book** is a set of paper pages that are glued or stitched together. Words and pictures may be printed on the pages. This dictionary is a book.

boot (noun)

A **boot** is a kind of shoe that covers your ankle. You wear boots outdoors to keep your feet warm and dry.

box (noun) plural **boxes**

A **box** is an object with four flat sides, a bottom, and sometimes a lid. You can keep things in a box.

bread (noun)

Bread is a type of food made with flour and baked in the oven. You can make toast from a slice of bread.

a bus

Bb

break (verb)
If you **break** something, it splits into smaller pieces or stops working.

breakfast (noun)
Breakfast is the first meal of the day. What did you eat for breakfast this morning?

breathe (verb)
To **breathe** is to take air into your body through your nose or mouth, then send it out again. The air that you breathe in and out is called your breath.

bridge (noun)
People build a **bridge** over a river, road, or railroad, so that they can cross easily to the other side.

brother (noun)
A boy who has the same mother and father as you is your **brother**. Do you have any brothers?

brush (noun) plural brushes
A **brush** is a tool with a handle and short, stiff hairs. You use different brushes to sweep the floor, paint, tidy your hair, or clean your teeth.

brush (verb)
To **brush** is to use a brush to do something. You brush your hair with a hairbrush.

building (noun)
A **building** is something with walls and a roof that someone has built. Houses, garages, stores, and factories are all buildings.

bus (noun) plural buses
A **bus** is a vehicle with lots of seats inside. It travels on roads and carries people from place to place. You wait for a bus at a bus stop.

busy (adjective)
If you are **busy**, you have a lot of things to do.

A place can be **busy**, too. A street is busy when there are lots of cars and people going by.

butterfly (noun) plural butterflies
A **butterfly** is a kind of insect with four wings. Some butterflies have white wings, but most are very colorful.

button (noun)
A **button** is something that you use to close up clothing, such as a shirt or a coat. You push a button through a buttonhole to hold two parts together.

Cc

cage (noun)

A **cage** is a container with bars. Some pets and zoo animals are kept in cages.

cake (noun)

A **cake** is a kind of sweet food that you bake in the oven. For your birthday, you may have a cake with candles on it.

camel (noun)

A **camel** is a mammal with one or two humps on its back. It lives in the desert.

camera (noun)

A **camera** is a machine that you can use to take photographs or make movies.

camp (verb)

To **camp** is to live in a tent for a short time. Have you ever been camping?

candle (noun)

A **candle** is a stick of wax with a piece of string that goes through the middle. When the string burns, a flame gives off light.

car (noun)

A **car** is a vehicle with an engine and wheels. People drive cars along the road.

carrot (noun)

A **carrot** is a plant with a long, orange root underground. The root is a sweet-tasting vegetable that we eat.

cartoon (noun)

A funny drawing in a newspaper or book is called a **cartoon**.

A **cartoon** is also a movie made with a series of drawings instead of real actors or animals. Donald Duck is a cartoon character.

castle (noun)

A **castle** is a large building with thick walls. Most castles were built long ago to protect people from their enemies.

a caterpillar

cat (noun)
A **cat** has soft fur, a long tail, and sharp claws. It is a mammal. Many people have pet cats. Tigers and lions are cats too, but they cannot be kept as pets.

caterpillar (noun)
A **caterpillar** looks a bit like a fat worm with lots of legs. Caterpillars turn into butterflies or moths.

cave (noun)
A **cave** is a large hole or tunnel in rock, either underground or in the side of a cliff or mountain.

cereal (noun)
A **cereal** is one of a group of plants whose seeds are used to make flour for bread, pasta, and other foods.

Cereal is also a breakfast food that many people eat with milk.

chair (noun)
A **chair** is a piece of furniture with a seat and a back. It is made for one person to sit on.

cheese (noun)
Cheese is a kind of food made from milk. There are lots of different kinds of cheese. What kinds do you like?

chicken (noun)
A **chicken** is a kind of bird that farmers raise for people to eat. Chickens lay eggs, which can also be used as food.

chip (noun)

A **chip** is a small piece broken off something, such as a cup or plate.

A **chip** is also a kind of salty snack, such as a potato chip.

A silicon **chip** is the tiny part inside a computer that makes it work.

chocolate (noun)

Chocolate is a sweet, brown flavoring for food. Many desserts and candies are made with chocolate.

city (noun) plural **cities**

A **city** is a very large town where lots of people live and work. London, Paris, and New York are cities.

classroom (noun)

A **classroom** is a place at a school where students go to learn.

climb (verb)

You **climb** when you move up or down something tall, such as a mountain, a ladder, or stairs.

clock (noun)

A **clock** is a machine that tells the time. Some clocks have two hands that move in a circle and point to the hours and minutes in a day. Other clocks use only numbers to show the time.

close (adjective)

If you are **close** to something, you are near it.

close (verb)

When you **close** something, you shut it.

clothes (noun)

You wear **clothes** to cover your skin and keep you warm.

cloud (noun)

Clouds are the white or gray shapes that float in the sky and hide the sun. Rain and snow fall from clouds.

Smoke or dust can form a **cloud** as well.

clown (noun)

A **clown** is someone who dresses up to look strange and colorful. He or she does funny things to make you laugh.

cold (noun)
If you have a **cold**, you feel sick and have to blow your nose a lot.

cold (adjective)
Cold is the opposite of hot. You feel cold in snowy weather.

a clown

color (noun)
Red, orange, blue, and green are **colors**. What is your favorite color?

computer (noun)
A **computer** is a machine that can store information and do many jobs. It can be used to tell what the weather will be like or to make traffic lights change color.

continent (noun)
A **continent** is a large piece of land with oceans around it.

count (verb)
To **count** is to say numbers in the right order.

You **count** things to find out how many there are.

country (noun) plural **countries**
A **country** is a part of the world with its own name, people, and laws. France and Canada are countries.

The **country** is also land that is not in a town or city. There are farms and open spaces in the country.

Cc

C c

cry (verb)

When you **cry**, tears fall from your eyes. You may cry if you are unhappy.

cut (noun)

A **cut** is an opening in your skin made by something sharp. It hurts!

cut (verb)

When you **cut** something, you slice it into pieces with a knife or a pair of scissors. You can cut a hole in something, too.

a crown

cousin (noun)

Your **cousin** is the child of your uncle or aunt.

cow (noun)

A **cow** is a mammal that lives on a farm and eats grass and hay. Cows give us milk to drink and meat to eat.

crocodile (noun)

A **crocodile** is a large reptile that lives near water in hot places such as Africa and Australia. It is a fierce hunter that uses its sharp teeth to eat other animals.

crown (noun)

Kings and queens wear **crowns** on their heads for special events. Crowns are usually decorated with gold and jewels.

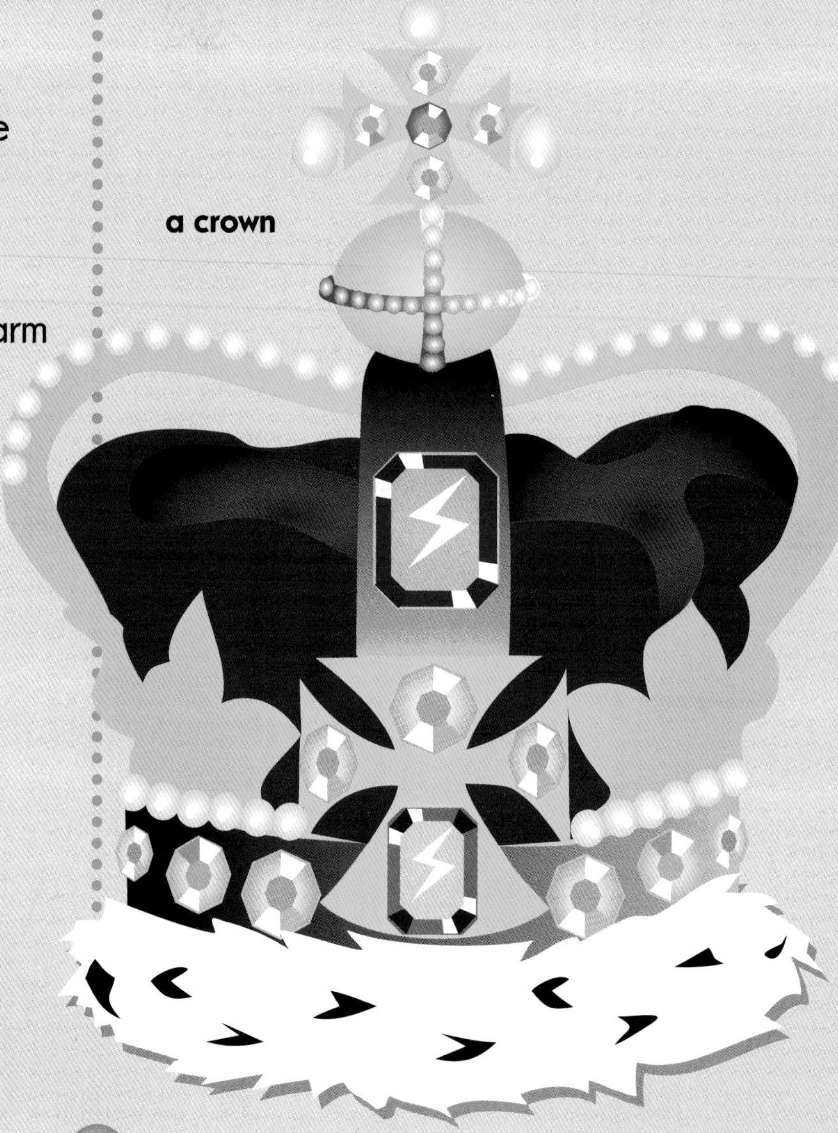

Dd

dance (verb)
When you **dance**, you move your body in time to music.

dark (adjective)
It is **dark** when there is no light. It is dark at night.

A color can be **dark**, too. A dark color, such as dark blue, is not pale.

date (noun)
A **date** is the day, month, and year when something happens. What date is your birthday?

A **date** is also a small, brown fruit with a hard seed inside it. It grows on a tree called a date palm.

day (noun)
A **day** is the 24 hours between one midnight and the next. There are seven days in a week.

It is called **day** when it is light outside.

deaf (adjective)
If you are **deaf**, you cannot hear sounds.

decide (verb)
To **decide** is to make a choice about something. You may have to decide whether to play a game or watch television.

dentist (noun)
A **dentist** is a doctor who takes care of your teeth. He or she checks to make sure they are healthy.

desert (noun)
A **desert** is an area on Earth that is very dry. Only certain kinds of animals and plants are able to live there.

desk (noun)
A **desk** is a table where you sit to write, draw, or use a computer. It may have drawers for storing things.

diamond (noun)
A **diamond** is a jewel that looks like clear glass. Some people wear diamonds in a ring or a necklace.

A **diamond** is also a shape. It looks a bit like a square standing on one of its corners (see page 63).

dictionary (noun)
plural **dictionaries**
This book is a **dictionary**. It tells you what words mean and shows you how to spell them.

difficult (adjective)

Difficult is the opposite of easy. It is difficult to rub your stomach and pat the top of your head at the same time!

dig (verb)

To **dig** is to make a hole in the ground. Some animals dig with their paws. Gardeners dig with a shovel.

dinosaur (noun)

Dinosaurs were large reptiles that lived millions of years ago. Some dinosaurs were huge. *Gigantosaurus* was the largest meat-eating dinosaur. It was nearly 50 feet (14 meters) long.

dirty (adjective)

If something is **dirty**, it is not clean. It may be covered with mud, dust, food, or other things.

discover (verb)

When you **discover** something, you find it or learn about it for the first time.

doctor (noun)

A **doctor** is someone who helps you get better when you are sick.

dog (noun)

A **dog** is an animal that many people keep as a pet. Dogs are mammals and are covered with fur. They wag their tails when they are happy to see you.

dolphin (noun)

A **dolphin** is a mammal that lives in water. It is smart and playful.

donkey (noun)

A **donkey** is a mammal that looks like a small horse with long ears.

door (noun)

A **door** a flat piece of wood, metal, or glass that you pull or push to enter a room or building. Cars and cupboards also have doors that open and close.

dragon (noun)

A **dragon** is an animal that you read about in stories. It is not real, but in stories it has a long tail and wings, and it breathes fire.

draw (verb)

To **draw** is to make a picture with a pen, pencil, or crayon.

dream (noun)

A **dream** is something that you seem to hear and see when you are asleep. It is not real.

dress (noun) plural **dresses**

A **dress** is a piece of clothing that girls and women sometimes wear. It covers the upper body and some or all of the legs. It is open at the bottom.

dress (verb)

To **dress** is to put on your clothes.

drink (verb)

When you **drink**, you swallow a liquid. You drink when you are thirsty. What do you like to drink best?

drop (noun)

A **drop** is a tiny bit of liquid, such as a drop of rain or a drop of blood. Drops of water sometimes drip from a faucet.

drop (verb)

If you **drop** something, you let it fall out of your hand.

dry (adjective)

Dry is the opposite of wet. If your hair is dry, there is no water in it.

a dinosaur

Dd

Ee

eagle (noun)

An **eagle** is a large bird with sharp claws and a hooked beak. Eagles catch and eat other animals.

Earth (noun)

Earth is the planet on which we live. It is round and travels around the sun. Most of Earth is covered with water. There are large areas of land, too.

The soil that plants grow in is also called **earth**.

easy (adjective)

If something is **easy** to do, you can do it without any problems. Easy is the opposite of difficult.

eat (verb)

When you **eat**, you put food in your mouth, chew it, and swallow it. You must eat food to stay alive.

egg (noun)

An **egg** is an oval or round object in which some young animals grow until they are ready to be born. Female birds lay eggs. Most female amphibians, fish, reptiles, and insects lay eggs, too.

Earth

electricity (noun)

Electricity is power that travels through wires into our homes. You use electricity when you switch on a light.

elephant (noun)

An **elephant** is a large mammal with a long nose called a trunk. Elephants live in forests and grassy areas of Asia and Africa. They can live for 70 years.

engine (noun)

Some machines have **engines**. This part makes power to run the machine. Cars have engines.

Europe (noun)

Europe is a large area of land. It is a continent. France and Spain are two of the many countries in Europe.

face (noun)
Your **face** is the front part of your head, from your forehead to your chin.

face (verb)
When you **face** something, you look toward it.

fall (verb)
To **fall** is to land suddenly on the floor or ground. You may hurt yourself.

family (noun) plural **families**
A **family** is a group of people made up of grandparents, parents, and children. Some families have aunts, uncles, and cousins, too. Who is in your family?

farm (noun)
A **farm** is a place where farmers grow plants or raise animals for food.

fast (adjective)
A **fast** runner runs quickly. Fast is the opposite of slow.

fat (adjective)
Fat is the opposite of thin. Someone who eats too much may get fat.

favorite (adjective)
When you like something best, it is your **favorite**. What is your favorite color?

feather (noun)
A **feather** is one of the long, thin objects that cover a bird's body. Feathers keep a bird warm and help it to fly through the air.

feel (verb)
You **feel** something when you touch it. It may feel rough or smooth.

You can also use the word **feel** to say how you are inside. You may feel happy or sad, tired or hungry.

fence (noun)
A **fence** is a kind of wall made of wood. metal, or wire. Some fences keep people out. Some fences keep animals in.

find (verb)
When you **find** something, you suddenly have something that you did not know was there. Find is the opposite of lose.

finish (verb)
When you **finish** something, you come to the end of it.

fire (noun)
A **fire** is the hot, bright light that comes from something that is burning. People sometimes make fires to keep themselves warm.

fire engine (noun)
A **fire engine** is a truck in which firefighters travel. A fire engine holds the tools that the firefighters need.

first (adjective)
Something that is **first** comes before all the others. The first letter of the alphabet is A.

fish (noun) plural **fish**
A **fish** is an animal that lives and breathes underwater. It is covered in scales, and it has fins and a tail that it uses for swimming.

fish (verb)
To **fish** is to try to catch a fish using a fishing rod or a net.

flavor (noun)
A **flavor** is what you taste when you eat food. What flavors do you like?

float (verb)
To **float** is to stay on the surface of a liquid instead of sinking. A duck floats.

To **float** also means to stay up in the air. Some balloons float away in the air if you let go of them.

flower (noun)
A **flower** is the part of a plant that makes seeds. Many flowers are brightly colored. Some smell beautiful.

fly (noun) plural **flies**
A **fly** is a small insect. It has one pair of see-through wings. There are many different kinds of flies.

fly (verb)
To **fly** is to move through the air. Flies and airplanes can fly. What else can you think of that flies?

food (noun)
You eat **food** to keep you healthy and make you grow. It tastes good, too!

friend (noun)
A **friend** is someone you like and who likes you. Friends are kind to you, and they are fun to be with.

frog (noun)

A **frog** is a small amphibian with smooth skin and long back legs. It lives near water and jumps to move around.

fruit (noun)

Fruit grows on trees or bushes and has seeds inside. Oranges, apples, and bananas are kinds of fruit.

funny (adjective)

Something that is **funny** makes you laugh. A joke is meant to be funny.

Something can also be **funny** if it is strange or odd, like a funny feeling.

fur (noun)

Fur is the fine, soft, hairy coat that keeps some animals warm. Cats and dogs have fur, but fish and birds do not.

Ff

a fish

Gg

game (noun)
A **game** is something that is fun to play. Soccer is a game.

garden (noun)
A **garden** is a piece of land where people grow flowers or vegetables.

gas (noun) plural **gases**
A **gas** is not a solid or a liquid. It is very light and you cannot see it. Air is a mixture of gases.

Gas is also a liquid fuel for cars and other vehicles. "Gas" is short for "gasoline."

gate (noun)
A **gate** is a door that you open to get to the other side of a fence. You must shut the gate to keep any animals from getting out.

giant (noun)
A **giant** is a very tall person that you read about in stories. Jack met a giant when he climbed the beanstalk.

giraffe (noun)
A **giraffe** is a mammal with a long neck and long legs. It lives in Africa.

give (verb)
If you **give** something to someone, you let him or her have it. It is fun to give a present to a friend.

a gorilla

glass (noun)

Glass is a hard material that you can see through. Windows are made of glass. Glass can break quite easily.

A **glass** (plural **glasses**) is also an object made of glass that you drink from.

glasses (noun)

Some people wear **glasses** in front of their eyes to help them see better.

glue (noun)

Glue is a liquid or paste that you use to stick things together.

go (verb)

To **go** is to move to or from a place. Where do you like to go best?

gold (noun)

Gold is a shiny yellow metal. Some jewelry is made of gold because it looks beautiful. Gold is very expensive.

goldfish (noun) plural **goldfish**

A **goldfish** is a small orange fish that some people keep as a pet. It is not made of gold!

gorilla (noun)

A **gorilla** is a kind of mammal called an ape. It is very large and black. It has long arms and can pick things up with its hands and feet. Gorillas live in Africa.

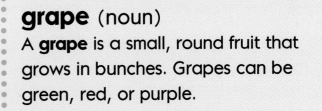

grape (noun)

A **grape** is a small, round fruit that grows in bunches. Grapes can be green, red, or purple.

greedy (adjective)

If you are **greedy**, you want more of something than you really need.

grow (verb)

To **grow** is to get bigger. You will grow as you get older.

If you **grow** flowers and vegetables, you plant them in soil and take care of them so they do not die.

guess (verb)

If you do not know the answer to a question, you can **guess**. Your guess may be right or wrong.

Hh

hair (noun)

A **hair** is a thin, thread-like material that grows out of your skin, especially on your head. What color is your hair?

hammer (noun)

A **hammer** is a heavy tool that people use to pound nails.

happy (adjective)

If you are **happy**, you feel cheerful. You may smile and laugh.

hat (noun)

A **hat** is a piece of clothing that you wear on your head.

healthy (adjective)

When you are **healthy**, you are not sick. Your body is fit and feeling well.

heavy (adjective)

If something is **heavy**, it weighs a lot. It is difficult to move.

hedgehog (noun)

A **hedgehog** is a small mammal with sharp spines all over its back. It rolls up into a ball to protect itself.

helicopter (noun)

A **helicopter** is a machine that can travel through the air. Instead of wings, it has blades on top that spin around.

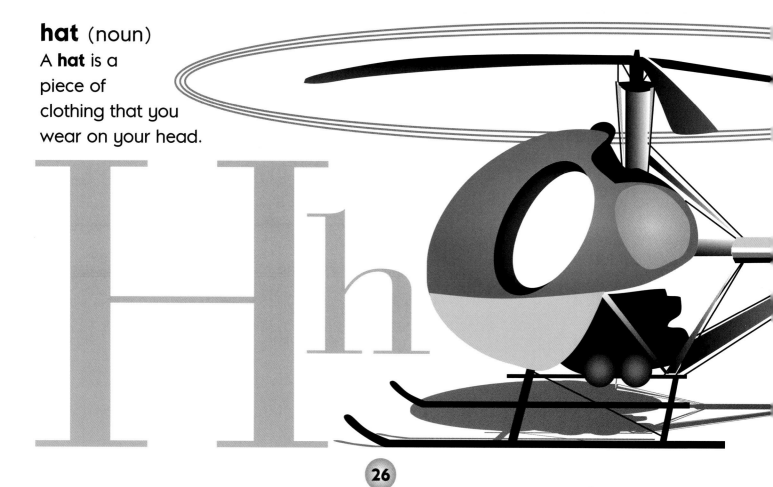

hide (verb)
When you **hide**, you go somewhere where you cannot be seen.

You can **hide** objects, too. Then nobody else can find them.

hill (noun)
A **hill** is an area of land that is higher than the land around it. It is smaller than a mountain.

hippopotamus (noun)
plural **hippopotamuses**
A **hippopotamus** is a mammal with short legs and a large body shaped like a barrel. It lives in Africa, where it likes to lie in muddy water to keep cool.

a helicopter

hit (verb)
To **hit** something is to strike it hard. Tennis players hit a ball with a racket.

holiday (noun)
A **holiday** is a day when you do not go to school or work. Many people hold special celebrations in honor of the day.

home (noun)
Your **home** is the place where you live.

horse (noun)
A **horse** is a mammal with a mane, a long tail, and hooves. People ride horses or use them to pull carts or carriages.

hospital (noun)
A **hospital** is a building you go to if you are very sick or badly hurt. Doctors and nurses at the hospital take care of you.

hot (adjective)
If you touch something very **hot**, you may burn yourself. Hot is the opposite of cold.

hour (noun)
An hour is a period of time. There are 60 minutes in an hour and 24 hours in a day.

hungry (adjective)
When you are **hungry**, you want something to eat.

ice (noun)
When water is very cold, it freezes hard and becomes **ice**.

iceberg (noun)
An **iceberg** is a huge piece of ice that floats in a cold ocean such as the Arctic.

ice cream (noun)
Ice cream is a frozen, sweet food made from cream or milk. Ice cream comes in many flavors.

idea (noun)
When you have an **idea**, you think of something. Your idea may be to play a game with your friends or read a book.

insect (noun)
An **insect** is a small animal with six legs. Beetles, flies, wasps, and butterflies are all insects.

island (noun)
An **island** is a piece of land with water all around it.

itch (noun) plural **itches**
If you have an **itch** on your skin, you may scratch it to make it stop itching.

jar (noun)
A **jar** is a container that you can keep things in. Jars are usually made of glass.

jewel (noun)
A **jewel** is a valuable stone, such as a diamond. People often wear jewelry, such as a necklace, made of jewels.

joke (noun)
A **joke** is something you say to make people laugh.

journey (noun)
A **journey** is a trip to a place far away.

juice (noun)
Juice is the liquid in fruit and vegetables. You squeeze an orange to make the juice come out.

jump (verb)
To **jump** is to leap into the air.

Jupiter (noun)
Jupiter is the biggest planet traveling around the Sun. It is more than ten times bigger than Earth.

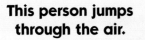

Jj

Kk

kangaroo (noun)

A **kangaroo** is a mammal that lives in Australia. It has strong back legs for jumping. A female kangaroo keeps her babies in a pouch on her stomach.

king (noun)

A **king** is a man from a royal family who is ruler of his country.

kite (noun)

A **kite** is a toy that you fly in the sky on a windy day. It is made of cloth or paper wrapped around a frame. You tie a string to it so it doesn't fly away.

knife (noun) plural **knives**

A **knife** is a tool with a long, sharp edge and a handle. You use a knife to cut things.

knock (verb)

To **knock** something is to hit or bump it. You knock on a door to find out if anyone is in the room.

knot (noun)

If you twist and tie two pieces of string or rope together tightly, you make a **knot**. A knot can be difficult to undo.

ladder (noun)

A **ladder** is a tall set of steps that you can carry from place to place. You climb a ladder if you want to reach something that is high up.

large (adjective)

Something that is **large** is big. Large is the opposite of small.

laugh (verb)

When you **laugh**, you make a sound to show that you think something is funny.

leaf (noun) plural **leaves**

A **leaf** is one of the flat parts of a plant. Most leaves are green. In the autumn, some leaves change color and fall off.

letter (noun)

Words are made up of **letters**. There are 26 letters in the alphabet.

A **letter** is also a message written on a piece of paper. You put a letter in an envelope and mail it to someone.

library (noun) plural **libraries**

A **library** is a place where you can go to read or borrow books.

light (noun)

The sun gives off **light**. A light bulb gives you light, too. You can turn on a light if it is dark, so that you can see.

light (adjective)

Light is the opposite of dark. It is light during the day.

A color can be **light**, too. A color such as light blue is pale.

Light is also the opposite of heavy. Something that is light does not weigh very much.

light (verb)

To **light** a fire is to make it begin to burn. People sometimes light a fire with a match.

lightning (noun)

Lightning is a flash of light you can sometimes see in the sky during a storm. You may hear thunder, too.

lion (noun)

Lions are large wild cats that live in Africa. A male lion has a thick mane. A female lion is called a lioness.

liquid (noun)

A **liquid** is something that you can pour or drink. Orange juice is a liquid. If you melt chocolate, it becomes liquid.

a lizard

Ll Ll

lizard (noun)

A **lizard** is a reptile. It has scaly skin. It has a long body and tail, a long tongue, and four legs.

look (verb)

If you want to **look** at something, you turn your eyes toward it to see it.

You also **look** for something that you have lost, if you want to find it.

lose (verb)

If you **lose** something, you don't have it anymore and you don't know where it is.

Lose is also the opposite of win. If you lose a game, someone else wins.

loud (adjective)

A **loud** sound is easy to hear because it is noisy.

love (verb)

If you **love** someone, you like that person very much.

Mm

It is magic when a magician makes a rabbit appear.

machine (noun)
People use **machines** to do jobs for them. Machines have lots of moving parts that work together. What machines do you have in your house?

magic (noun)
In stories, **magic** is the power used to make impossible things happen.

In real life, **magic** is when someone does clever tricks that seem impossible.

make (verb)
You **make** something if you create something new.

mammal (noun)
A **mammal** is an animal with fur or hair. It feeds its young on milk. Dogs, horses, lions, and humans are all mammals.

map (noun)
A **map** is a drawing that shows you where places are.

Mars (noun)
Mars is one of the nine planets that circle the sun. Mars is sometimes called the red planet.

mask (noun)
People wear **masks** over their faces to protect them or hide them. You may wear a mask when you want to pretend to be someone else.

medicine (noun)
If you are sick, the doctor may give you **medicine**. This medicine is often liquid or pills. It will make you feel better.

melt (verb)
When something solid **melts**, it becomes liquid. Heat makes things melt. When ice melts, it becomes water.

Mm

mend (verb)

If something is broken or torn, you **mend** it so that you can use it again.

Mercury (noun)

Mercury is one of the nine planets that circle the sun. It is the one that is closest to the sun.

metal (noun)

A **metal** is a hard material such as iron, gold, or silver. These metals are found in the ground. People use metals to make things like cars and jewelry.

middle (noun)

The **middle** of an area is the center. It is the place farthest away from all the edges.

milk (noun)

Milk is the white liquid that a female mammal makes in her body to feed her baby. People often drink cows' milk.

minute (noun)

A **minute** is a short period of time. There are 60 seconds in a minute and 60 minutes in an hour.

mirror (noun)

If you look in a **mirror**, you can see yourself. A mirror is made of shiny glass.

mix (verb)

To **mix** is to put different things together. If you mix two paint colors, you make a different color.

mobile (adjective)

If something is **mobile**, you can move it. Lots of people have a mobile phone, which they carry around with them.

money (noun)

Money is the coins and pieces of paper that people use to buy things.

monkey (noun)

A **monkey** is a mammal that lives in forests in hot countries. It uses its arms, legs, and tail to swing through the trees.

monster (noun)

A **monster** is a scary creature you read about in stories. Monsters are not real.

month (noun)

A **month** is a period of time. There are 31 days in most months, but some are shorter. There are 12 months in one year. In what month is your birthday?

moon (noun)

The **moon** is like a small planet, but it circles Earth instead of the sun. You can see it in the sky at night.

morning (noun)

The **morning** is the first half of a day, before 12 o'clock, or noon.

mouse (noun) plural **mice**

A **mouse** is a small mammal with a furry body, a long thin tail, and a pointed nose. Some people keep mice as pets.

Mm

A **mouse** is also something you use to move things on a computer screen.

move (verb)

If you **move**, you do not stay still. You can move part of your body, such as your finger. You can also move yourself or an object from one place to another.

mud (noun)

Mud is wet, sticky soil. Your shoes will get muddy if you walk in mud.

a mouse on a mouse

name (noun)

People call you by your **name**. Places have names, too, such as England and California. What is your name?

necklace (noun)

A **necklace** is a piece of jewelry that you wear around your neck.

Neptune (noun)

Neptune is one of the nine planets that circle the sun. It is cold and windy.

nest (noun)

A **nest** is a home built by some animals for their babies to live in. Birds' nests are often made of grass and straw.

new (adjective)

If something is **new**, it has not been used yet. A new coat is one that you have just bought.

newspaper (noun)

A **newspaper** is made up of large sheets of paper folded together. It has stories about what is happening in the world.

night (noun)

Night is the time when it is dark outside.

noisy (adjective)

If something is **noisy**, it is very loud. It makes a lot of noise. Music can be noisy. So can people!

North America (noun)

North America is a large area of land. It is a continent. The countries called the United States of America and Canada are both in North America.

number (noun)

You use **numbers** when you count. Numbers can be written as words or as special signs. One (1) and two (2) are numbers. Which number comes next?

nurse (noun)

A **nurse** is someone who takes care of people who are sick or hurt. Many nurses work in hospitals or clinics.

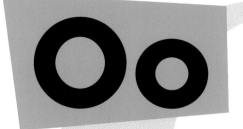

Oo

ocean (noun)

An **ocean** is a very large sea. The Pacific Ocean is the largest ocean in the world.

octopus (noun) plural **octopuses**

An **octopus** is an animal that lives in the sea. It has eight long arms called tentacles, which it uses to catch food.

oil (noun)

Oil is a thick, smooth liquid. You can cook with oil that comes from plants. Some oil comes from deep inside Earth. People burn this to make heat.

old (adjective)

If something is **old**, it was made a long time ago. Old is the opposite of new.

An **old** person is someone who has lived a long time.

open (adjective)

If something is **open**, it is not shut. A door can be open. So can your mouth.

open (verb)

If you want to go into a room, you **open** the door.

orange (noun)

An **orange** is a type of fruit. It has thick, orange skin that you peel off so that you can eat the flesh inside.

oval (noun)

An **oval** is a shape, like a circle that has been squashed a little (see page 63).

owl (noun)

An **owl** is a bird that hunts mostly at night. It has large eyes that help it see in the dark.

Pp

package (noun)
A **package** is something wrapped in paper or sealed in a box. You may get a package in the mail on your birthday.

page (noun)
Each sheet of paper in a book is called a **page**.

pain (noun)
Pain is a feeling you have in a part of your body if you have hurt yourself or if you are sick.

paint (noun)
Paint is a colored liquid that you use with a brush to make pictures. You can also brush paint on a door or a wall to change its color.

paint (verb)
To **paint** is to use paint to make a picture or change the color of something.

pair (noun)
Two things that are the same and go together are called a **pair**. Socks come in pairs. Shoes come in pairs, too.

panda (noun)
A **panda** is a large, furry mammal that lives in bamboo forests in China. It is black and white, with black around its eyes. There are not many pandas left.

paper (noun)
Paper is a thin material usually made from wood. The pages in this book are made of paper. You can write and draw on paper, or wrap presents in it.

an octopus

parent (noun)

Your mother and father are your **parents**. The parents of your parents are your grandparents.

park (noun)

A **park** is an area where everyone can go to play or excercise. There may be trees, swings, or baseball fields.

park (verb)

To **park** is to leave a car somewhere. People often park in a parking lot.

parrot (noun)

A **parrot** is a colorful bird with a large, curved beak. Wild parrots live in forests in hot countries. Others are kept as pets. Parrots learn to copy sounds and words.

party (noun) plural **parties**

A **party** is a special time when you and your friends have fun together. Do you like going to parties?

pedal (noun)

A **pedal** is part of a machine that you press with your foot to make the machine work. There are two pedals on a bicycle.

pencil (noun)

A **pencil** is a thin, wooden stick that you use for writing and drawing. Pencils may have gray, black, or colored lead.

penguin (noun)

A **penguin** is a bird that lives near the sea. It cannot fly, but it uses its small wings to swim through the water. Most penguins live in Antarctica.

period (noun)

A **period** is a dot that is used to show where a sentence ends.

pet (noun)

A **pet** is an animal that lives with you in your home. Many people have a pet cat, dog, or hamster.

photograph (noun)

A **photograph** is a picture that you take with a camera.

piano (noun)

A **piano** is a large musical instrument. It has a keyboard with black and white keys that you press with your fingers to make music.

picnic (noun)

A **picnic** is a meal that you take away from home and eat outdoors.

piece (noun)

A **piece** is a bit of something.

pig (noun)

A **pig** is a mammal that is kept on a farm for its meat. It has a curly tail.

pirate (noun)

A **pirate** is someone who attacks and robs ships at sea. There are lots of stories about pirates.

a pirate

pizza (noun)

A **pizza** is a flat, round piece of bread covered with cheese, tomatoes, and other foods. It is baked in the oven.

planet (noun)

A **planet** is a large, round object in space that circles around a large star. Earth is a planet. It circles around a star we call the sun.

plant (noun)

A **plant** is a living thing with a stem, leaves, and roots. A tree is a plant. A flower is a plant, too.

plastic (noun)

Plastic is a material made in factories. Soda bottles and toys are some of the things that can be made of plastic. Plastic can be difficult to break.

P p

If you jump in a puddle, your feet may get wet.

play (noun)

A **play** is a story that is acted out by people. You can watch a play at a theater, or you can make up one with your friends.

play (verb)

To **play** is to have fun. You can play games with your friends or by yourself.

You also **play** a musical instrument to make music.

Pluto (noun)

Pluto is a planet. It is the smallest of the nine planets that circle the sun.

poem (noun)

A **poem** is a piece of writing laid out in several short lines. Often the words at the ends of each line rhyme.

polar bear (noun)

A **polar bear** is a large, white mammal that lives in the Arctic, where the sea and land are covered in snow and ice.

police (noun)

The **police** are men and women whose job is to keep us safe and make sure that people obey the law.

pond (noun)

A **pond** is a small area of water. Some people have a pond in their garden.

poor (adjective)

Someone who is **poor** does not have very much money.

You can use the word **poor** if you feel sorry for someone. You might say, "Poor baby, you must be hungry."

post (noun)

A **post** is a pole fixed in the ground. A post can be made of wood, metal, or a kind of stone called concrete.

potato (noun) plural **potatoes**

A **potato** is a round vegetable. It is the part of the potato plant that grows underground. Do you like potatoes mashed, fried, or baked?

pour (verb)

To **pour** is to make a liquid flow from one container to another. You might pour juice from a pitcher into your glass.

president (noun)

The **president** is the person chosen to lead a group of people. In the United States, a president is chosen every four years.

pretend (verb)

If you **pretend**, you try to make people believe something that is not true. Can you pretend to be asleep?

prince (noun)

A **prince** is the son of a king or queen.

princess (noun)

plural **princesses**

A **princess** is the daughter of a king or queen, or the wife of a prince.

prize (noun)

You may win a **prize** if you do well in a contest or a game.

promise (verb)

If you **promise** to do something, it means you really will do it. If you don't do it, you break your promise.

puddle (noun)

A **puddle** is a small pool of liquid. You may see puddles of water on the ground after it rains.

pull (verb)

If you **pull** something, you move it toward you.

push (verb)

If you **push** something, you move it away from you.

put (verb)

To **put** something somewhere is to move it to that place.

Qq

quarter (noun)
A **quarter** is a large, silver coin worth 25 cents. Four quarters equals one dollar.

queen (noun)
A **queen** is a woman from a royal family who is ruler of her country. The wife of a king is also called a queen.

question (noun)
When you want to find out something, you ask a **question**. Usually, someone will give you an answer that tells you what you want to know.

quick (adjective)
Quick is another word for fast. A frog has to be quick to catch an insect.

quiet (adjective)
Quiet is the opposite of loud. You must be quiet if you do not want anyone to hear you.

quilt (noun)
A **quilt** is a blanket made by sewing together small pieces of fabric.

quit (verb)
To **quit** is to stop doing something.

Rr

rabbit (noun)
A **rabbit** is a mammal that has long ears, sharp front teeth, and a short, fluffy tail. It lives in burrows that it digs in the ground. Many people keep rabbits as pets.

radio (noun)
A **radio** is a machine that allows you to hear sounds that come from a long way away. You can use a radio to listen to music or news reports.

railroad (noun)
A **railroad** is a set of metal tracks on which trains travel to take people and things to different places.

rain (noun)
Rain is the water that falls to the ground in drops from clouds in the sky.

rainbow (noun)
A **rainbow** is a band of colors that you sometimes see in the sky after it rains. It is made up of seven colors: red, orange, yellow, green, blue, indigo (a reddish blue), and violet (purple).

rat (noun)
A **rat** is a mammal with sharp teeth and a long tail. It is bigger than a mouse.

read (verb)
To **read** is to look at written words and understand what they mean. Can you read the words in this book?

remember (verb)
If you **remember** something, you think of it again.

rain forest (noun)
A **rain forest** is a thick, wet forest that is usually found in hot places. Millions of different animals, such as butterflies, parrots, and snakes, live in a rain forest.

reptile (noun)
A **reptile** is an animal with scaly skin that lays eggs. Snakes, lizards, crocodiles, and turtles are all reptiles.

a rainbow

rhinoceros (noun)
plural **rhinoceroses**

A **rhinoceros** is a large, heavy mammal that lives in Africa and southern Asia. It has one or two horns on the end of its nose and thick, wrinkly skin.

ribbon (noun)

A **ribbon** is a long piece of material that you may use to tie up a present. Some girls tie ribbons in their hair.

rice (noun)

Rice is a food made from the seeds of rice plants. You cook the seeds to make them soft and fluffy.

ride (noun)

A **ride** is a short journey on a bicycle or horse, or in a car.

You may go on a **ride**, such as a Ferris wheel, at a theme park. Some rides are very scary.

ride (verb)

When you **ride** a bicycle, you sit on it and make it move along. Some people ride horses and ponies, too.

ring (noun)

A **ring** is a thin band that you can wear around your finger.

A **ring** is also a circle.

ring (verb)

You **ring** a bell to make a sound. You ring a doorbell on a house to let the people inside know that you are there.

ripe (adjective)

If something is **ripe,** it is finished growing and is ready to eat. A banana turns yellow when it is ripe.

river (noun)

A **river** is a stream of water that starts in the hills and flows down to the sea.

road (noun)

A **road** is a wide path for cars, bicycles, and buses to drive on. It may be made of dirt, rocks, or a black material called tar.

roar (verb)

To **roar** is to make a loud, deep noise. Lions and tigers roar. The sound of lots of traffic or a waterfall can be called a roar, too.

robot (noun)

A **robot** is a machine that can do a job that is usually done by a person. Robots make many things in factories.

rocket (noun)

A **rocket** is a powerful engine that puts spacecraft into space.

roller skate (noun)

Roller skates are boots with wheels on the bottom for skating over hard, smooth ground.

roof (noun)

A **roof** is the covering on top of a building or car. It protects the building from the rain and the sun.

rope (noun)

A **rope** is a very thick piece of string. It is made of lots of threads twisted together to make it strong.

round (adjective)

Something that is **round** is shaped like a circle (see page 63) or a ball.

run (verb)

When you **run**, you move your legs faster than you do when you walk. You must run as fast as you can if you want to win a race.

A tiger opens its mouth to roar.

Ss

sad (adjective)

If you are **sad,** you feel bad and may cry. Sad is the opposite of happy.

safe (noun)

A **safe** is a strong metal box with a lock. People keep things, such as money and important papers, inside it.

safe (adjective)

If something is **safe**, nothing can hurt it. Old photographs will be safe in a safe!

salt (noun)

Salt is a white powder that some people put on their food to give it more flavor. Salt is taken from the ground or from seawater.

sand (noun)

Sand is dry soil made of tiny bits of rock and shell. You can find sand on a beach and in the desert.

sandwich (noun)
plural **sandwiches**

A **sandwich** is two pieces of bread put together with another type of food, such as cheese, between them. What type of sandwich do you like best?

Saturn (noun)

Saturn is one of the nine planets that circle the sun. Millions of pieces of rock and ice travel in rings around it.

school (noun)

School is where children go to learn lots of different things. At school, there are teachers to teach you and help you. Many adults go to school, too.

scissors (noun)

Scissors are like two knives joined together in the middle. You use scissors to cut things.

sea (noun)

A **sea** is a large area of salty water. It is smaller than an ocean. When the sea is rough, it has large waves in it.

seal (noun)

Seals are mammals that live in the sea as well as on land. They have flippers instead of feet and are very good swimmers.

second (noun)

A **second** is a very short period of time. There are 60 seconds in a minute.

second (adjective)

If you finish **second** in a race, one person was faster than you. That person was first.

Ss

see (verb)
To **see** is to use your eyes to look at something.

sew (verb)
To **sew** is to use a needle and thread to join pieces of cloth together.

shadow (noun)
A **shadow** is the dark shape you make when you stand in front of a light or the sun.

shark (noun)
A **shark** is a large fish that lives in the sea. Sharks have lots of sharp teeth. Most sharks eat smaller fish and seals.

sharp (adjective)
Something that is **sharp** has a point or edge that can cut or prick you easily. A thorn and a knife are sharp.

sheep (noun) plural **sheep**
Sheep are animals kept on farms for their wool and meat. The wool is used to make clothes.

shell (noun)
A **shell** is a hard covering, like the outside of an egg or a nut. Animals such as turtles also have a shell.

ship (noun)
A **ship** is a large boat. It carries people and things to other countries.

shoe (noun)
You wear **shoes** on your feet to protect them from sharp objects and to keep them warm and dry.

a ship

47

shop (verb)

To **shop** is to look for things to buy.

shout (verb)

To **shout** is to speak very loudly. People shout when they are mad or when they are talking to someone who is far away.

shovel (noun)

A **shovel** is a tool with a long handle and a flat blade for digging.

shower (noun)

When you take a **shower**, you wash yourself under a spray of water.

A short rainstorm is called a **shower**, too.

shut (verb)

When you **shut** something, you use a cover, lid, or door to block an opening.

silver (noun)

Silver is a shiny, gray metal. People use silver to make jewelry.

size (noun)

The **size** of something is a measurement of how big or small it is.

skateboard (noun)

A **skateboard** is a small board on wheels. You stand on it and push off with one foot to make it go. Some people can even do tricks on a skateboard.

skin (noun)

You have **skin** all over the outside of your body. It helps protect your body from water and germs. Fruit and vegetables have a skin, too.

sky (noun)

The **sky** is the space above Earth, where you can see the sun during the day and the moon at night.

sleep (verb)

To **sleep** is to close your eyes and rest. You go to sleep when you are tired. When you are asleep, you do not notice what is happening around you.

slide (verb)

To **slide** is to move smoothly on a surface. You can slide on ice.

slide (noun)

A **slide** is a type of toy that you can play on. It has a long, slippery, slope that you slide down.

slow (adjective)

If you are **slow**, you take a long time to do something, or you do not move quickly. Slow is the opposite of fast.

small (adjective)

Something that is **small** is not large. A mouse is small. So is a kitten. They are both smaller than a horse.

a snake

Ss

soap (noun)
You use **soap** with water to wash yourself, your clothes, or the dishes. Soap makes bubbles.

solid (adjective)
A **solid** object is hard and firm.

Something that is **solid** has no air in the middle.

song (noun)
A **song** is a piece of music with words that you sing.

The musical sound that some birds make is also called a **song**.

snake (noun)
A **snake** is a long, thin reptile that has no legs. It slithers along the ground on its belly. Some snakes give poisonous bites that can kill you.

snow (noun)
Flakes of **snow** are small pieces of frozen water. Snow sometimes falls from the sky when it is very cold.

soup (noun)
Soup is a liquid food with pieces of vegetables or meat in it.

South America (noun)
South America is a large area of land. It is a continent that is joined to North America.

space (noun)

A **space** is an empty area between objects. You need lots of space to play football.

Space is also everything beyond Earth, where all the stars and planets are.

spacecraft (noun)

A **spacecraft** is a machine that travels into space. A space shuttle is a spacecraft.

speak (verb)

To **speak** is to say words.

spell (noun)

A **spell** is a group of magic words that makes things happen. Witches often cast spells in fairy tales.

spell (verb)

To **spell** is to put letters in the right order to make a word. How do you spell your name?

spider (noun)

A **spider** is a small animal with eight legs. It is not an insect, because insects have only six legs.

a spider

spill (verb)
If you **spill** your drink, you let it fall out of the cup by mistake.

splash (verb)
To **splash** is to make drops of liquid move through the air. If you splash in the bathtub, the floor may get wet.

spring (noun)
Spring is the time of year that comes after winter and before summer. It gets warmer and brighter in spring, and plants start to grow.

A **spring** is a curly wire that you can squeeze together. When you stop squeezing, it will spring back to its first shape.

A **spring** is also a place where water comes out of the ground and becomes a stream.

spring (verb)
To **spring** is to jump suddenly.

squeak (verb)
To **squeak** is to make a short, high sound, like the sound a mouse makes. Doors and machines often squeak, too!

squirrel (noun)
A **squirrel** is a mammal with a bushy tail. It lives in trees and eats nuts.

stamp (noun)
A **stamp** is a sticky piece of paper that you put on a letter. The stamp shows that you have paid to mail your letter.

A **stamp** is also an object used to print a mark on paper. You may get a stamp on your passport when you enter another country.

stamp (verb)
To **stamp** is to bang your foot down on the ground.

star (noun)
You can see **stars** in the sky at night. They are millions of miles away.

A shape with points is called a **star** (see page 63).

A famous person is also called a **star**. Who is your favorite movie star?

start (verb)
When you **start** to do something, you begin to do it.

stone (noun)
A **stone** is a small piece of rock.

The hard seed inside some fruits is called a **stone**. Peaches and plums have a stone inside them.

stop (verb)

When you **stop** doing something, you do not do it anymore. If something becomes still, it **stops**. A bus stops at a bus stop.

You can also **stop** something or someone other than yourself. If you stop the music, you turn it off so it does not play anymore.

storm (noun)

A **storm** is very bad weather. There is a strong wind and lots of rain or snow. There may be thunder and lightning.

story (noun) plural **stories**

A **story** tells you about things that have happened, or things that a writer has made up for fun. You can read or listen to a story, and often there are pictures too.

street (noun)

A **street** is a road in a town or city that has houses or buildings on each side of it.

string (noun)

String is strong, thick thread that you use to tie things together.

Some musical instruments have **strings** that you touch to play notes. These strings are usually made of wire.

strong (adjective)

A person who is **strong** is powerful and can lift heavy things. Strong is the opposite of weak.

A **strong** object is hard to break.

A **strong** smell is easy to sense.

summer (noun)

Summer is the time of year when the weather is warmest. Summer comes after spring and before autumn.

sun (noun)

The **sun** is the star that Earth and the other planets circle. The sun gives us light and heat. You can often see the sun in the sky during the day.

surprise (verb)

If you **surprise** people, you do or say something they did not expect.

swing (noun)

A **swing** is a seat that hangs from ropes or chains. It is fun to sit on a swing and swing back and forth.

swing (verb)

To **swing** is to move from side to side or backward and forward through the air.

Tt

table (noun)
A **table** is a piece of furniture with legs and a flat top.

tadpole (noun)
Tadpoles are baby frogs, toads, or newts, which are amphibians. Tadpoles have long tails and live in water.

tail (noun)
The long, thin part at the end of an animal's body is called a **tail**. A dog wags its tail if it is happy to see you.

talk (verb)
To **talk** is to speak to someone.

teach (verb)
To **teach** is to show someone how to do something. You have teachers at school who teach you different things.

telephone (noun)
A **telephone** is a machine that you can use to talk to people far away.

tadpoles

telescope (noun)
A **telescope** is a tube-shaped tool that makes things look closer and larger. You use a telescope to look at the stars.

television (noun)
A **television** is a machine with a screen. It receives signals that it changes into moving pictures with sound.

tent (noun)

A **tent** is a small shelter made of strong cloth. Poles and ropes hold it up. You sleep in a tent if you go camping.

thirsty (adjective)

If you are **thirsty**, you want something to drink.

throw (verb)

To **throw** is to use your hand to send something through the air.

thunder (noun)

Thunder is the loud rumbling noise you sometimes hear during a storm. You may see lightning, too.

tickle (verb)

When you **tickle** someone, you touch or poke them gently with your fingers to make them laugh.

tiger (noun)

A **tiger** is a mammal. It is a large, wild cat with orange and black striped fur. Tigers live in forests in Asia.

time (noun)

Time is the passing of years, months, days, hours, minutes, and seconds.

A particular moment during the day is also called the **time**. You tell the time with a clock or a watch.

tire (noun)

A **tire** is a ring of rubber that fits around a wheel. Most tires are filled with air. Cars and bicycles have tires.

today (noun)

Today is this day. What day is it today?

tomorrow (noun)

Tomorrow is the day after today.

tooth (noun) plural **teeth**

A **tooth** is one of the hard white objects in your mouth that you use to bite and chew. When you are young, your first set of teeth fall out and new teeth grow.

tough (adjective)

Something that is **tough** is strong and able to bend without breaking. Meat that has cooked for too long can be tough to chew.

A **tough** person is able to handle hard times without complaining.

town (noun)

A **town** is a place where there are stores, houses, schools, and offices. It is smaller than a city.

toy (noun)

A **toy** is something you play with.

Tt

tractor (noun)
A **tractor** is a strong machine with large wheels. Farmers use tractors to pull other machines and heavy loads.

traffic (noun)
Cars and trucks going along the road are called **traffic**. Sometimes there is a traffic jam and the traffic cannot move.

train (noun)
A **train** is a a string of cars pulled by an engine along a metal track. It carries people or things from place to place.

train (verb)
To **train** is to teach a person or an animal a special skill or job.

treasure (noun)
Treasure is a collection of gold, silver, jewels, or other valuable things.

A teddy bear is a toy.

tree (noun)
A **tree** is a tall plant with branches, leaves, and a thick, wooden stem.

trumpet (noun)
A **trumpet** is a musical instrument made of metal. You blow into it to play music.

55

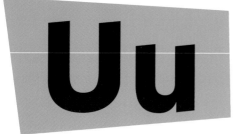

Uu

umbrella (noun)
An **umbrella** is a circle of cloth stretched over a metal frame. It has a long handle so that you can hold it up over your head to protect you from the rain or the sun.

uncle (noun)
If your mother or father has a brother, he is your **uncle**. The husband of your aunt is your uncle, too.

understand (verb)
To **understand** is to know what something means or how it works.

unhappy (adjective)
If you are **unhappy**, you are not happy. You feel sad or upset.

unicorn (noun)
A **unicorn** is an animal that you read about in stories, but it is not real. It looks like a white horse with one horn growing from the front of its head.

a unicorn

universe (noun)
The **universe** is everything in space. All the planets, stars, and moons are part of the universe.

Uranus (noun)
Uranus is a planet that circles around the sun. It is covered in a thick layer of blue gas.

valley (noun)
A **valley** is an area of low ground between hills or mountains.

van (noun)
A **van** is a long, tall car with extra seats or empty space in the back. People use vans to carry people and deliver things.

vegetable (noun)
A **vegetable** is a kind of food that grows on a plant. Carrots, lettuce, broccoli, and potatoes are vegetables.

vehicle (noun)
A **vehicle** is any machine that carries things or people from place to place. Boats, bicycles, airplanes, and trains are all vehicles.

Venus (noun)
Venus is one of the nine planets that circle around the sun. It is the closest planet to Earth.

vet (noun)
A **vet** is an animal doctor who helps animals get better when they are sick. "Vet" is short for "veterinarian."

violin (noun)
A **violin** is a small musical instrument made of wood, with wire strings. You move a special stick called a bow across the strings to make sounds.

visit (verb)
To **visit** is to go to see a person or place.

voice (noun)
Your **voice** is the sound you make when you speak or sing. Everyone's voice sounds a little bit different.

volcano (noun) plural volcanoes
A **volcano** is a mountain that has hot melted rock, gases, and ash inside it. Sometimes, these hot things shoot out of the top of the volcano.

vote (verb)
To **vote** is to choose something or someone. You may write your choice on a piece of paper or raise your hand to be counted.

vulture (noun)
Vultures are large birds that feed on dead animals. Most vultures do not have any feathers on their heads.

walk (verb)
To **walk** is to move along by putting one foot in front of the other.

wall (noun)
A **wall** is one of the sides of a building or room.

A **wall** can also separate one piece of land from another. It is like a fence, but it is made of stones or bricks.

warm (adjective)
Something that is **warm** is a little hot but not hot enough to hurt you.

wash (verb)
When you **wash** something, you clean it with soap and water.

water (noun)
Water is a liquid that you can drink. It comes out of the faucets in your house. You can use this water for cooking and washing, too. Ocean water is too salty to drink.

water (verb)
You **water** plants in dry weather by adding water to the soil around them.

weather (noun)
The **weather** is what it is like outside. It may be hot or cold, rainy or sunny.

week (noun)
A **week** is a measure of time that is seven days long. There are 52 weeks in a year.

whale (noun)
A **whale** is a mammal that lives in the sea. The blue whale is the largest animal that has ever lived.

wheel (noun)
A **wheel** is a round object that turns or rolls. Cars, bicycles, and trains move along on wheels.

win (verb)
If you **win** a race, you finish first. You may be given a prize when you win.

wind (noun)
Wind is air that is moving quickly. The wind moves leaves and branches.

wind (verb)
To **wind** something is to twist it around something else. You wind thread around a spool.

You **wind** a key in some toys and clocks to make them work.

A road **winds** if it has lots of bends.

word (noun)

A **word** can be written or spoken. It is a group of letters or sounds that mean something. This book is full of words.

worm (noun)

A **worm** lives in the ground. It is a long, thin animal with no legs. Worms are found all over the world.

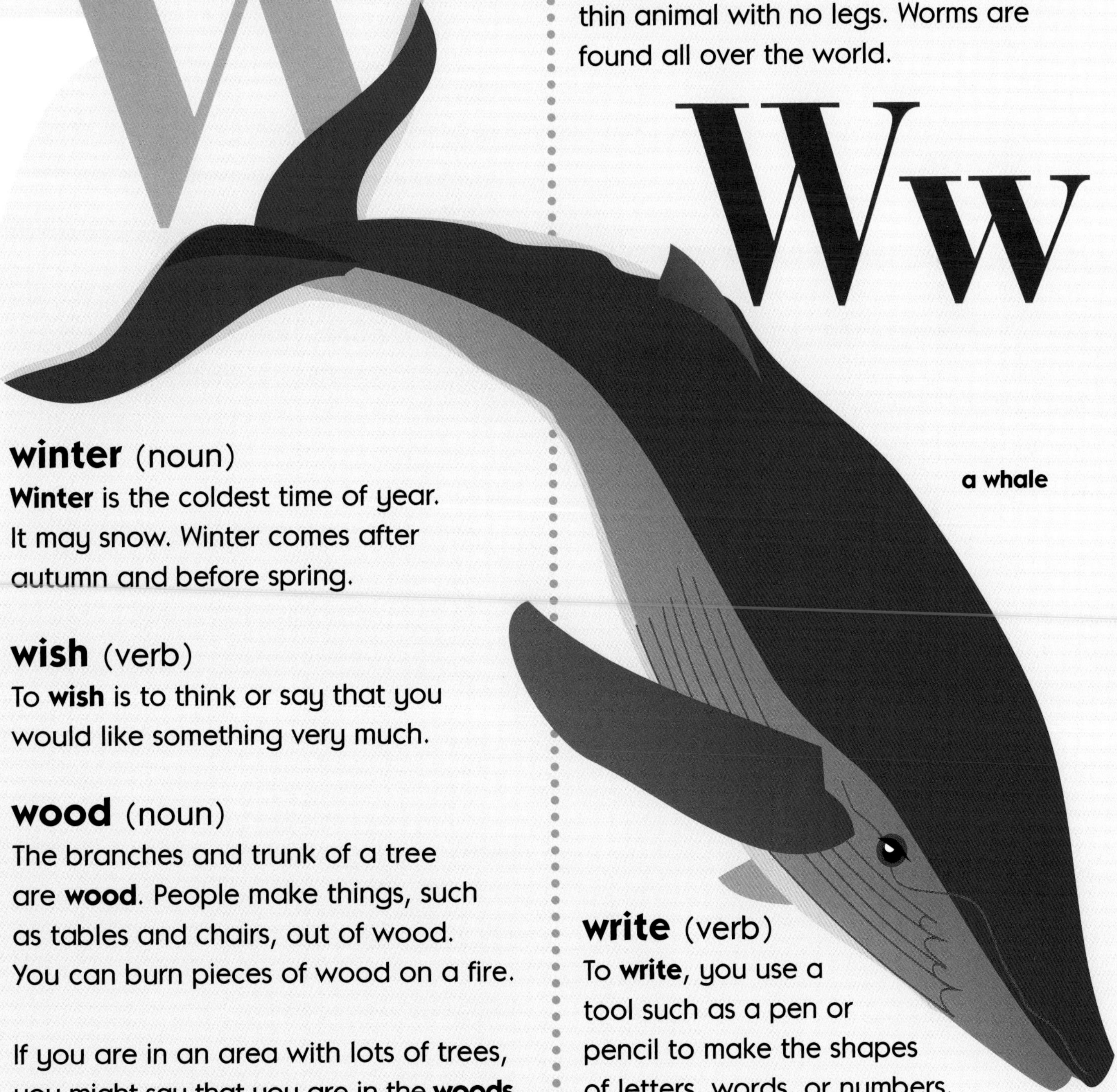

W w

a whale

winter (noun)

Winter is the coldest time of year. It may snow. Winter comes after autumn and before spring.

wish (verb)

To **wish** is to think or say that you would like something very much.

wood (noun)

The branches and trunk of a tree are **wood**. People make things, such as tables and chairs, out of wood. You can burn pieces of wood on a fire.

If you are in an area with lots of trees, you might say that you are in the **woods**.

write (verb)

To **write**, you use a tool such as a pen or pencil to make the shapes of letters, words, or numbers.

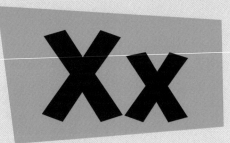

x-ray (noun)

An **x-ray** is a photograph of the inside of a person's body. Doctors look at x-rays to find out if a person has a broken bone or an illness.

xylophone (noun)

A **xylophone** is a musical instrument with a set of wooden or metal bars. You hit the bars with one or two special sticks to play different notes.

yacht (noun)

A **yacht** is a large, fancy boat used for racing or sailing.

yak (noun)

A **yak** is a mammal that looks a little like a cow with a shaggy coat. It lives in the mountains of Asia.

yawn (verb)

When you **yawn**, you open your mouth wide and breathe in deeply. You may yawn when you are tired.

year (noun)

A **year** is a measure of time. It is the time it takes Earth to circle the sun. There are 12 months in a year.

yell (verb)

To **yell** is to shout or scream very loudly.

yesterday (noun)

The day before today was **yesterday**. Did you go to school yesterday?

yogurt (noun)

Yogurt is a sour food made from milk. Yogurt often has fruit in it.

yolk (noun)
The yellow part of an egg is the **yolk**.

young (noun)
An animal's babies are often called its **young**.

young (adjective)
An animal or person that is **young** has lived for only a short time.

yo-yo (noun)
A **yo-yo** is a small toy. When you play with a yo-yo, you make a wheel move up and down a piece of string.

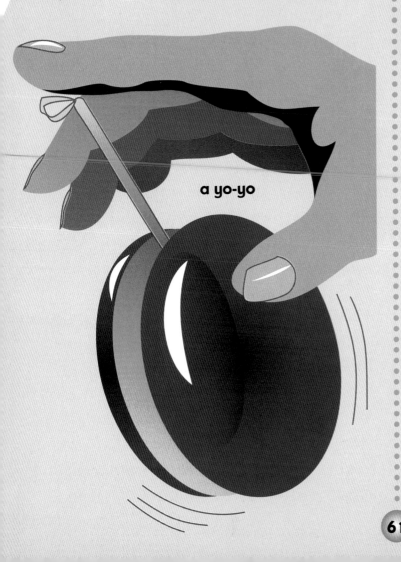

a yo-yo

zebra (noun)
A **zebra** is a mammal that looks like a black and white striped horse. Zebras live on the grassy plains of Africa.

zigzag (noun)
A **zigzag** is a line with lots of sharp, pointed turns.

zigzag (verb)
To **zigzag** is to move forward making short, sharp turns from side to side.

zipper (noun)
A **zipper** is made of two sets of metal or plastic teeth that join together. You zip up the opening in some clothes and bags with a zipper.

zoo (noun)
A **zoo** is a place where lots of different wild animals are kept. You can go to see the animals in a zoo.

ZZZzz

Some Useful Words

 one
 two
 three
 four
 five

six   seven   eight   nine   ten

Numbers

one	1	sixteen	16
two	2	seventeen	17
three	3	eighteen	18
four	4	nineteen	19
five	5	twenty	20
six	6	thirty	30
seven	7	forty	40
eight	8	fifty	50
nine	9	sixty	60
ten	10	seventy	70
eleven	11	eighty	80
twelve	12	ninety	90
thirteen	13	one hundred	100
fourteen	14	one thousand	1,000
fifteen	15	one million	1,000,000

Days of the week

Monday	Friday
Tuesday	Saturday
Wednesday	Sunday
Thursday	

Months of the year

January	July
February	August
March	September
April	October
May	November
June	December

Colors

yellow

blue

green

red

pink

black

gray

orange

brown

purple

Shapes

square

rectangle

oval

circle

star

diamond

triangle

Index

This index will help you find some of the words in this dictionary. The numbers are the pages where you will find them.

animals
amphibian 6
animal 7
ant 7
bear 8
bee 8
bird 9
butterfly 11
camel 12
cat 13
caterpillar 13
chicken 13
cow 16
crocodile 16
dinosaur 18
dog 18
dolphin 18
donkey 18
eagle 20
elephant 20
fish 22
fly 22
frog 23
giraffe 24
goldfish 25
gorilla 25
hedgehog 26
hippopotamus 27
horse 27
insect 28
kangaroo 29
lion 30
lizard 31
mammal 32
monkey 33
mouse 34
octopus 36
owl 36
panda 37
parrot 38
penguin 38
pet 38
pig 38

polar bear 40
rabbit 42
rat 43
reptile 43
rhinoceros 44
seal 46
shark 47
sheep 47
snake 49
spider 50
squirrel 51
tadpole 53
tiger 54
vulture 57
whale 58
worm 59
yak 60
zebra 61

food and drink
apple 7
banana 8
bread 10
breakfast 11
cake 12
carrot 12
cereal 13
cheese 13
chicken 13
chip 14
chocolate 14
date 17
egg 20
food 22
fruit 23
grape 25
ice cream 28
juice 28
milk 33
orange 36
pizza 39
potato 41
rice 44

sandwich 46
soup 49
vegetable 57
water 58
yogurt 60

in space
Earth 20
Jupiter 28
Mars 32
Mercury 33
moon 34
Neptune 35
planet 39
Pluto 40
Saturn 46
space 50
star 51
sun 52
universe 56
Uranus 56
Venus 57

on Earth
Africa 6
Antarctica 7
Arctic 7
Asia 7
Australia 7
cave 13
continent 15
country 15
desert 17
Europe 20
hill 27
island 28
North America 35
ocean 36
rain forest 43
river 44
sea 46
South America 49
valley 57
volcano 57

people
astronaut 7
aunt 7
baby 8
brother 11

clown 14
cousin 16
dentist 17
doctor 18
friend 22
king 29
nurse 35
parent 38
pirate 39
police 40
president 41
prince 41
princess 41
queen 42
uncle 56
vet 57

transportation
airplane 6
bicycle 9
boat 10
bus 11
car 12
fire engine 22
helicopter 26
railroad 42
rocket 45
ship 47
spacecraft 50
tractor 55
traffic 55
train 55
van 57
yacht 60

weather
autumn 7
cloud 14
lightning 30
rain 42
rainbow 42
shower 48
snow 49
spring 51
storm 52
summer 52
thunder 54
weather 58
wind 58
winter 59